APPLE VALLEY YEAR

by Ann Turner

illustrated by Sandi Wickersham Resnick

MACMILLAN PUBLISHING COMPANY   NEW YORK   MAXWELL MACMILLAN CANADA   TORONTO

MAXWELL MACMILLAN INTERNATIONAL   NEW YORK   OXFORD   SINGAPORE   SYDNEY

BY THE SAME AUTHOR

Dakota Dugout
Grasshopper Summer
Hedgehog for Breakfast
Nettie's Trip South
Third Girl from the Left
Tickle a Pickle
Time of the Bison

Author's note: Mice can eat enough bark from apple trees to damage the trees. Foxes eat the mice, and so help keep the orchard healthy.

Text copyright © 1993 by Ann Turner
Illustrations copyright © 1993 by Sandi Wickersham Resnick
All rights reserved. No part of this book may be reproduced or transmitted in any form or by any means, electronic or mechanical, including photocopying, recording, or by any information storage and retrieval system, without permission, in writing from the Publisher. Macmillan Publishing Company is part of the Maxwell Communication Group of Companies. Macmillan Publishing Company, 866 Third Avenue, New York, NY 10022. Maxwell Macmillan Canada, Inc., 1200 Eglinton Avenue East, Suite 200, Don Mills, Ontario M3C 3N1. First edition. Printed in the United States of America. The text of this book is set in 16 pt. Espirit Book. The illustrations are rendered in acrylics.

10 9 8 7 6 5 4 3 2 1

Library of Congress Cataloging-in-Publication Data. Turner, Ann Warren. Apple Valley year / by Ann Turner ; illustrated by Sandi Wickersham Resnick. — 1st ed.   p.   cm. Summary: The Clark family keeps busy through all four seasons at their apple orchard, pruning dead branches at the end of winter, carrying the beehives among the trees in May, propping up branches heavy with summer fruit, and harvesting the apples in the fall. ISBN 0-02-789281-6 [1. Orchards—Fiction. 2. Seasons—Fiction.] I. Resnick, Sandi Wickersham, ill. II. Title. PZ7.T8535Ap 1993   [E]—dc20   90-37733

For Judy, with love, for her patience and support
—A. T.

To my parents, Jeff and Eva Wickersham
—S.W.R.

Before the sap flows, Ralph Clark harnesses his two great Belgian horses and drives them up the hill to his apple orchard. The winter horseshoes strike sparks on the road.

Ralph takes out his shears and clips away the winter-dead branches. He burns them in a pile, gray smoke curling into the blue sky. "Good pruning makes good apples," Mr. Clark tells the horses as he loads logs cut last fall onto the sledge.

A fox plays on the brow of the hill, leaping and pouncing on meadow mice grown bold by the lengthening sun. She is so fast, no one would know she is carrying new kits inside.

In Sarah Clark's kitchen, Tim and Martha sip hot cocoa and do their schoolwork at the table. When their father comes in, knocking snow from his boots, he says:

"I saw the fox in the orchard." He holds out his hands to the stove. "She'll keep those pesky mice down."

"I wish I could see her," Martha says. "Maybe this summer."

In May, when the fox in the orchard sleeps close to her kits, Ralph Clark harnesses his horses. He puts blinders on them so they won't be nervous.

He puts on his bee hat and veil and lights a fire in the smoker. He puffs smoke into his hives until the bees are sleepily still. His oldest sons move the hives onto the wagon, and slowly they drive to the apple orchard.

They set the beehives down among the trees. The blossoms are just opening—white, with pink edges. They smell like candy. When the bees awake, they will fly in and out of the blossoms. "Plenty of bees make good apples," Mr. Clark tells his sons.

"And good honeycomb," one answers.

Tim and Martha lie on their backs on a blanket in the field. They look for shooting stars and see two arching down the black sky. Martha wishes on one, "Let me see the foxes that live in Papa's orchard." Tim wishes for a new pair of leather boots.

Come summer, the blossoms drop, and in their place is the smallest idea of an apple, a tiny, green speck. The fox that lives in the orchard teaches her kits how to hunt. They are learning how to wait by a mouse's nest before they pounce.

One cloudy August day, the whole family walks
to the orchard. From a large pile they take strong,
Y-shaped sticks and put them under branches hanging
low with fruit. They sit on a rock and watch the apples
as the rain begins to fall. The trees are covered with
red-green balls. "Rain at the right time makes sweet
apples in the fall," Ralph says.

Tim and Martha set off for school in too-small shoes. "When we sell the apples," Martha says, "we will have new shoes."

"*You* will have shoes. *I* will have boots."

"Maybe," Martha says and swings her lunch pail.

On a cool September morning, Ralph Clark and his oldest sons drive the horses and wagon to the apple house set deep in the hill. They load wooden barrels onto the wagon. Tim and Martha paint their names on two of the round sides. Everyone climbs on the wagon, and they ride up to the orchard.

They unload the barrels throughout the orchard and set apple ladders that end in a point against the trees. Everyone picks apples into canvas sacks tied round their waists and then unloads them into the barrels. Martha looks for the foxes, but cannot see them hiding under a ledge.

Sarah Clark and Martha set out ham sandwiches and lemonade in the meadow under the trees at noon. "A good crop," they all agree. When they drive home at dusk, the wagon rumbles with the full barrels. Mr. Clark makes another trip before all the apples are put into the cool apple house. Some he will keep for the family to eat throughout the winter; the rest he will sell.

When the apple man comes, Ralph Clark opens the doors to his apple house and helps load the barrels. He gives the money to his wife to keep in the cash box under the bed.

Before snow comes and the ground freezes, the foxes can hunt. The new ones toss mice high in the air and pounce on chipmunks who hide in the long stone walls. Mr. Clark tells his family, "A fox in the orchard means good apples next year."

Mrs. Clark buys new leather shoes for Martha, with ten buttons on each one. Tim gets his high, black boots and smiles at his sister. She smiles back.

On a cool, quiet fall day, Ralph Clark harnesses the Belgian horses. He and his oldest sons drive the winding road to the orchard. Mr. Clark lights his smoker and puffs smoke into the hives until the bees are sleepily still.

He and his sons load the hives onto the wagon and drive slowly home. They set them with their backs against a hill facing south. The winter sun will keep the bees from freezing. Ralph takes trays of honey out of each hive, cutting off thick slabs of dripping honeycomb to store in the pantry. The rest he leaves for the bees. "Strong bees make good apples," he tells his wife.

Snow comes. The pond freezes over. Tim and Martha and the rest of the family get out their skates and make looping patterns on the ice. The foxes sleep longer days. Mr. Clark pries the summer shoes off his horses and nails on the winter shoes. One night after supper, Sarah Clark counts again the money in the cash box from the fall apples. "A good apple sale makes a good year." She smiles at her family.

Snow settles on the apple trees, piling on the
bare branches. The fox sleeps in the orchard. She will
be carrying new kits inside when Mr. Clark once again

harnesses his Belgian horses and sets out
to prune the winter-dead branches.